juan

by Mary Stolz

pictures by Louis S. Glanzman

HARPER & ROW, PUBLISHERS

New York, Evanston, and London

JS 876 ju

JUAN

Some Other Books by Mary Stolz

This is for Eileen and Joanie

chapter

one

Rumor flew through the orphanage like a breeze through the jacaranda trees. It set the children rustling and whispering together.

A party.

A party?

Well, that's what someone had said. There was going to be a party.

When?

Nobody knew.

Where?

No one knew.

Who knew there was going to be a party at all?

Nobody knew. But the rumor flew among them, and they rustled and whispered and remembered the other times.

There had not been many. Concepción, who had been in the orphanage since the day of her birth, sixteen years before, could recall five occasions when people from other worlds had arrived in the small Mexican town and, for one reason or another, had given a party for the orphanage children.

"Why do they do it?" Juan asked Concepción.

He wanted, more than anything else (except for maybe a pair of red rubber boots) for there to be a party. But Juan was curious about things, and he wondered why someone who didn't know them would give them a party.

"Because they're kind," said Concepción.

Juan looked at her steadily, saying nothing.

"Because they're sorry for orphan children."

Juan scowled. "I am not an orphan."

"But Casa María is the orphanage," Concepción explained. "How should strange people know that everybody in it isn't an orphan?"

"But why do they want to give us a party?" Juan persisted.

"Because they have lots and lots of money and don't know what to do with it."

Juan nodded. That seemed to make sense. "Is there going to be a party this time?" he asked.

Concepción didn't know.

"Tell me about the other times."

"Well, once there was a lady from Brazil.

That was before you were born," Concepción said to Juan, who was eight. "She was tall and skinny and beautiful. She wore gold filigree earrings and a silk dress printed with daisies—"

Juan moved impatiently. "What was the *party* like, Concepción?"

"Oh, lovely. Lovely. They took us in buses all the way out to the fields, and we had a lot to eat, and ball games, and—"

Oh, the fields, the fields!

They were green and grassy, sprawling in sunlight, and they stretched, Juan thought, to the world's edge. Heaven, Juan knew, was a field stretching all across the sky, where some of his friends, like Pablo Ortiz, were already playing.

"Will they take us to the fields this time?" he asked Concepción.

"We don't know if there's going to be a this time."

"I forgot. Yes, but somebody *said*."

"Who?"

Nobody knew. It was just a rumor that rustled among them and no one knew how it had started.

chapter
two

Once, oh a very long time ago, Concepción had been eight years old. Skinny as a root, with black hair and dark shining eyes, she had lived at Casa María as long as she could remember, and as long as she could remember, she had worked.

Since all of the girls at the orphanage, except the very little ones, worked too, Concepción saw no reason to wish it otherwise.

Certainly she wished for some things. For sweets to eat. For some way to make the court-yard sunny. For, although she knew this was foolish of her, some times to be alone.

But what she wished for mostly was someone of her own. There were children in the orphan-age who had brothers and sisters with them.

Some had relatives who visited now and then. Some even had a parent living, and though for reasons none of the children understood they couldn't live with this parent, they could, once in a while go and stay in a house they could properly call their own.

Concepción had no one.

Sister Angela, who was good and kind and tried to be a mother to all the children, couldn't be a mother, really, to any one of them. The Cura, Father Antonio, wasn't fatherly at all. He, along with the eight terrifying old ladies who made up "The Board," was the head of Casa María, although Sister Angela ran it. It was Concepción's opinion that Father Antonio didn't like the orphanage, or orphans, even though he called them, "My children," and patted their heads if someone was looking.

Concepción had no one, and it caused a pain around her heart that didn't go away even when she was happy. And she thought she was happy. Pretty happy. Most of the time. Well, some of the time.

One day in July, the year she was eight, Concepción was sent to the market to get flowers for the little chapel at Casa María.

"Two pesos' worth," said Sister Angela, handing Concepción the money. "And see that what you get is fresh. Last time the flowers wilted in a day. No, no," she added, at Concepción's expression. "It was not Carmina's fault, child, nor yours. Just tell Señora Velas at the flower stand that last time she did not offer her best to God and the orphanage."

"Yes, Sister Angela," said Concepción, bobbing. "I will tell her." She hesitated. "Just me, Sister? Not Carmina, too?"

Her impassive face hid the flow of joy and thankfulness she felt at this chance—to be sent alone, trusted to buy the flowers even though she and Carmina had last time not done very well. Carmina was much older, but not much wiser than Concepción, and Señora Velas had betrayed them.

But not this time, thought Concepción, her heart beating quickly, proudly.

She looked up at Sister Angela, who returned a question in her gaze.

She's done this for me, for a special grace, Concepción thought. To give me a chance to be alone for a little while. She wondered how Sister Angela had known what this meant to her.

Suddenly, surprising them both, Concepción seized Sister Angela's hand and kissed it. "Oh thank you," she breathed. "Thank you."

"It's all right, little one," said Sister Angela. "I'm—it's all right."

Concepción went, hurrying because it was the rainy season and almost two o'clock. But happy, happy as she could ever remember being.

Every day, in this hill town, during the summer, the sun would shine all morning, and then at just about two o'clock, great clouds would assemble darkly in the west, thunder would roll like wooden carts down the hills, and as if from an overturned bucket the rains would come.

Concepción delivered the two pesos and Sister Angela's message to Señora Velas, who lifted her eyes and her hands and swore that never, on her mother's grave, would she give less than her best to God and the orphanage.

"It must be," she said, giving Concepción an armload of snapdragons and daisies that were scarcely wilted at all, "that you delayed too long getting them into water."

Concepción knew this had not been so. She began to protest, but after all said nothing. She was eight years old, and Señora Velas was maybe a hundred and had a bad temper besides. Looking over her purchase, she decided it was good —better than most they had at Casa María. She hoped Sister Angela would understand that she'd done her best.

She had almost reached Casa María, when curtains of rain came driving and jostling out of the sky. In minutes the cobbled streets were cascades of water, and everyone on them rushed to find shelter.

Concepción darted toward the great wooden doors of Casa María, her hand already raised to lift the knocker and summon help to let her in out of the downpour.

Then she stopped, staring down, flowers dropping from her arms to scatter on the rain-ridden street.

A baby was lying in the doorway.

He was quite naked, and screaming with rage. Concepción stooped and picked up the slippery little body. He stretched and struggled so violently that for a moment she couldn't let go of him to reach the knocker. Finally, clutching him against her so tightly that he bawled louder than before, she quickly banged the knocker up and down.

After a long minute, the door creaked heavily open and there stood Sister Angela herself.

"Why—why, Concepción. In the name of the Virgin, what is this?"

Concepción stared up, looked down.

"I guess it's a baby, Sister Angela."

chapter
three

"Yes, yes," said Sister Angela. "I can see it is a baby. Come in, come in, Concepción." She glanced at the flowers, scattered and crushed by the rain, past saving. "Come in," she repeated briskly.

She led the way to her office, Concepción following with the furious infant in her arms.

"Adela," Sister Angela called to a passing girl. "Adela, bring towels, and some baby clothes. Quickly, quickly. Don't delay, child. Do as you're told."

Adela ran off.

"Now, Concepción."

"Now, Sister?" said Concepción blankly. She was quite wet and somewhat chilled, but she held the baby closely in spite of his screaming determination to escape her grasp. What a bony, powerful small thing he was.

"Where did you find this little one?" Sister Angela said, taking a towel from Adela. "Here, give him to me. Concepción—give me the baby."

"I can dry him, Sister. I'll do it."

Sister Angela's mouth opened, then closed. She handed the towel to Concepción and began to sort through the infants' wear that Adela had brought. Clothing that had been worn by many infants and would be worn by many more.

"Diaper, shirt, sweater. That should be enough. For now. I asked you a question, Concepción."

"He was in the doorway, Sister. Just lying there. Hollering."

Sister Angela sighed and shook her head. "Poor little thing. A foundling. Like Pablo."

Pablo Ortiz had been left, like this one, lying in the doorway of Casa María, a couple of years before.

"But I don't see," said Concepción, lifting her voice over the baby's continued clamor, "how anyone could do such a thing. Look at him, Sister Angela. He's so beautiful. How could anyone —just leave him? How could they do that?"

"Who knows?" Sister Angela's voice was weary. "Perhaps his mother is dead. Maybe his father, too. Or perhaps they can't afford to feed him. People know that here the children will, at any rate, be fed. That they'll get some schooling. And affection. At least," she said, looking at Concepción, "I hope the children feel they get affection here."

"Oh, yes. Yes, Sister," Concepción said quickly. "Yes we do. Feel that."

It was true. Sister Angela had great warmth and fondness for the orphans, and they all sensed it. The only trouble was that she had to stretch her affection over so many of them that any one of them felt sort of thinly covered.

Adela had been sent for a warm bottle of milk, and now when she returned with it, offered to feed the baby herself.

"I'll do it," said Concepción fiercely.

Again Sister Angela seemed about to protest, and again said nothing. She watched as Concepción settled in a chair, held the baby gently in her arms, held the bottle expertly for him to feed. A girl of Concepción's age had by now, at Casa María, learned most of what there was to know about caring for the young.

He sucked noisily, clenching and unclenching his fists, curling and uncurling his toes, jerking his legs with fury that gradually diminished as he realized that he was warm and being held and fed.

Sister Angela and the two girls watched as he

12

drained the last drop of milk and then slumped against Concepción's chest, exhausted, asleep.

At that moment, Father Antonio came into the office, his black soutane flapping wetly around his shoes.

"Why are all those flowers scattered out front?" he demanded.

Sister Angela and Adela stood up. Concepción, holding the now warm sleeping baby against her, hardly noticed the Cura. She was conscious of voices, but distantly, indifferently. Absorbed in an entirely unfamiliar, shakily sweet sensation, she rocked gently from side to side, and began to croon.

The Cura looked from Concepción and the baby to Sister Angela.

"Is this child sick? Why is he being attended to here, in your office?" He made it sound as if the shabby room were being, in some way, misused. "And why are all those flowers lying around outside?"

"Concepción here dropped them when she found the infant."

"Found? *Found?* Found him where? Send someone out to collect those flowers." He looked at Adela, who ran gratefully from his presence to gather up the sodden flowers that later appeared drooping on the chapel altar.

"I'm afraid we have another foundling,

Father," said Sister Angela.

Father Antonio put a hand to his forehead. "Another mouth to feed! What do these people think we are?"

"The orphanage," said Sister Angela, her voice humble. "Perhaps his mother died, and the father could think of nothing else to do. Perhaps—" She shrugged. There were so many possibilities, and what did they matter? Here the child was.

The Cura's jaw worked, and he bit his lip. "It is God's will," he said reproachfully. "We must bear it."

"Yes, Father."

"Was there a name attached to him, as in the case of the last one? Pablo, his name is?"

"Pablo Ortiz. No, Father Antonio. This baby was naked."

"Pah. Didn't care enough about him to cover his nakedness, or leave him a name. What people these are."

"Our people," said Sister Angela, very low. "Your flock."

"Yes, Sister," he snapped. "I am aware of that. But sometimes I think our people are—my flock is—" He looked at Concepción, and decided not to share his thought. "Well, call him Juan."

"Juan what?"

Father Antonio waved his hand. "Just Juan."

I guess he thinks you're lucky to get a name at all, Concepción said silently to her little burden. But when the Cura, more and more vexed, had departed, she said to Sister Angela, "Couldn't we call him Juan Rivera?" Concepción's own surname was Rivera.

"We'll see," said Sister Angela, looking tired.

But somehow Juan, except in Concepción's mind, never did have a last name. He was Juan. Even to himself. Just Juan.

chapter
four

As he grew, Juan continued his early promise of being powerful, beautiful, and angry. He wasn't angry all of the time, but his bad temper lay just beneath the surface of his good temper and could be touched off by any number of things, even when he didn't want it to be.

Sometimes Concepción called him her "Little Turtle," because when he wanted not to face a person, or a fact, or a fear, he withdrew into a shell of smoldering silence and could not be prodded forth until he himself decided to come forth.

One thing that enraged him, one fact he would not accept, was that he was an orphan.

He refused to be one.

He explained that he'd been stolen by bandits

and left there in the doorway because they didn't want to carry him in the rain. He said his parents were looking for him all over Mexico, and it was just a question of when they would find him, and then they would take him away from Casa María to his own house.

Sometimes his parents were on a long trip but would be back to claim him. He never said when. Just that one day they would. All of his stories ended with his departure from Casa María, which incensed Father Antonio, who wanted to believe that the children loved their orphanage. He had warned Juan not to continue making up such stories, and after each warning, Juan thought up a new one.

"You'd leave me?" Concepción would ask sadly.

"No, no," Juan would growl. "You come, too."

"But suppose they—your parents—don't want me?"

"They'll *want* you."

Once a man and his wife from Mexico City had come to Casa María and said they wished to adopt a child. This had thrown the orphanage into great turmoil, as no one except Sister Angela could remember when it had happened before. To be adopted was a matter none of them ever really thought about, because it was something that didn't happen.

Yet there it was, apparently about to happen.

Señor and Señora Mendoza stayed in the town and every day they came to Casa María and looked the children over. It was a nervous period, as the children were required to dress in their best and instructed not to get dirty. This was especially hard on the boys who, after church and school in the morning, had nothing to do. They got in one another's way and grew listless or short-tempered.

The girls fared better, as they were occupied, and so seemed more attractive. Nevertheless, after the first couple of days the Mendozas looked mostly at Juan. By now he was so handsome that even the Cura would look at him sometimes and say, "What a child, what a child," as if Juan were son to one of the bright fallen angels.

Said by the Cura, this did not come out to a compliment.

Concepción went about in a stony daze. She knew they would take him, and she would lose him, for how could anyone who wanted to adopt a child resist Juan?

And then, quite suddenly, they went away, taking no child with them. Sister Angela looked stern and confused, but would talk about the matter with no one, not even Concepción.

"It is better so," was all she would say.

Concepción, thinking to console Juan, who had perhaps been hoping for the great thing to happen to him, the adoption into a family, where he would be able to say, "Good morning, Papá," "Good night, Mamacita," like somebody's true child, went to him and pulled him close.

"Don't grieve," she said. "Don't grieve, my little Juan."

Juan had looked up at her slyly. "I wouldn't go with *them*," he said. "I'm waiting for my parents."

"But—" Concepción began, "but maybe—perhaps—" She couldn't bring herself to say it, but Juan interpreted her meaning.

"No," he said with dignity, pulling out of her arms. "When my mother and father come, I will know them and they will know me. Right away. That is how it will be. *Those* looked all around at everybody. You saw, Concepción. *My* mother and father will look at me right away and never look at anyone else."

"But they liked you. I thought they were going to—" She looked at him sharply. "Juan, what did you do? Did you say something to Señora Mendoza, when she was talking with you yesterday? What did you say to her?"

Still with that sly expression, Juan fixed his eyes dreamily upon the ceiling, where a great cockroach was crawling. "Nothing, Concepción." He added, after a moment, "Next to nothing."

"The next to nothing. Will you tell me what that was?"

Juan lifted his shoulders. "I said to the lady that she had a belly like a sick burro and if she took me with her I'd run away, and I told her I ate live frogs and wet the bed every night and used curse words."

Concepción put a hand to her mouth to stifle a giggle, but she felt it her duty to chide him. "That was very bad of you, Juan. Señora Mendoza was a nice lady. How could you say such things?"

But the turtle had gone into his shell and nothing more could be gotten from him.

chapter
five

Long before Juan was born, an artist visiting the little town had painted murals on the walls of the dormitories of Casa María, one at the end of the boys' domitory, one at the end of the girls'.

These rooms were high, narrow, and almost lightless despite a window over each great wooden door. Once the walls had been white-washed, but now were greyish, flaky, fly-spotted, and, here and there, lightly encrusted with moss. The murals, in their original state, had been brilliantly colored. Even now, years later, Juan found them glowing, beautiful.

The girls had a dark Madonna, surrounded by children. She held the baby Jesus in her rebozo, and had a spiked and golden halo over her head. The boys' mural showed Christ sitting like a bus driver at the front of a pink cloud, with children for passengers scattered behind him.

One early afternoon, before the rumor about the picnic had even started, Juan reclined on his mattress on the floor. At night he shared it with Emilio and little Luiscito, but now he had it all to himself.

He studied the fine painting on the wall, thinking it would be fun to ride along on a cloud behind the Lord Jesus, if you didn't have to die first to do it. He wondered if Pablo Ortiz, who had died last year, was now riding on a pink cloud with the Lord driving him.

Pablo had been lively as a jumping bean and always laughing about something.

"Stop scowling, Juan," he'd say. "Anyway, until you have something to scowl about."

"Don't I have?" Juan would ask, really wanting to know. It seemed to him he had plenty.

"No, not yet," Pablo told him once. "Wait till you're as old as I am. *Then* you'll have things to scowl about."

"Why don't you, then?"

But Pablo shrugged and laughed again. "Things could be worse, things could be worse."

Things had got worse for Pablo, and now he was dead, from some sickness that came and went fast. It had taken two of the babies, too. Juan guessed they were all in heaven now, and

he hoped they were happy.

He moved restlessly on the mattress, wishing there were something to do. School was over for the day, and just now there was no one else in here. The boys were out in the courtyard, playing soccer, and Juan could have been with them, but he didn't want to be. There wasn't enough room to run, not enough room to make a real soccer game.

There was always something for girls to do. They cooked and mended and did the laundry and took care of the babies and—ah well, they did lots of things. None of it was anything Juan wanted to do, but at least the girls stayed busy.

"Juan!"

Concepción was calling from the hall.

"Juan, are you in there?"

He didn't answer. Not that he didn't wish to. He couldn't. Silence, at times, was an enemy with a strong hand over his mouth. He could struggle, and move his lips, but no sound came against that muffling palm. So he sat on the mattress, listening, hoping she'd come and find him and make him talk.

"Juan, answer me!"

But he didn't, and he thought she'd gone away, but then, with a sigh of relief, he saw her coming toward him between the rows of triple-deck bunks and the mattresses on the floor.

"Now what are you doing?" she said briskly. "In here sulking by yourself."

"I'm not sulking."

"What then?"

"I think I'm thinking."

Concepción smiled a little. "Don't you want to play soccer?"

"No."

The orphanage children, boys and girls, were good soccer players. Except for Emilio, who was clumsy, the children were excellent at shooting the ball around from head to foot to knee, fast and hard. It was their favorite game in the courtyard. Even in the playground most of them preferred it to the swings, because there was room in the playground to run.

But both the courtyard and the playground were paved with brick, and Juan could remember what it had been like to play on grass. He had been to the fields only once, last year on the Cura's name day, when the children of Casa María had been taken on a picnic by Father Antonio and "The Board," none of whom had gone along.

It had been the happiest day of his life, and Juan decided now that he would rather go back there even than have a pair of red rubber boots.

"What are you thinking about?" Concepción asked.

"Pablo, I guess."

"I see."

There was nothing Concepción could think of to say about Pablo. He'd been a merry little boy, he was gone, and they missed him.

But death was very much a part of life in Mexico. Even in so small a town, almost every week there was a funeral. Big ones with many mourners, and maybe a band. Little ones, unnoticed except for the sad-faced father carrying a little coffin, his wife walking silently behind with the other children, grieved and yet glad that this little one was now in heaven, and safe. Old people, babies, boys like Pablo died. Dogs died and were left lying in the street until somebody got around to carting them off. Pigs, led squealing by a rope around one leg, were dragged through the streets and you knew what was going to happen to them. And, on Sunday, the Cura told about how everyone, saint and sinner —except according to him they were all sinners —would one day be summoned by the Angel of Death so they'd better be in a state of grace at all times in case the call was sudden, as in Pablo's case.

In Mexico, children got sugar skulls with their names on them for holidays. They ate candy skeletons. They knew about Death, and sometimes made a sweetmeat of Him.

26

"I miss Pablo, too," said Concepción, wanting to share Juan's unhappiness.

"I didn't say I missed him. I said I was thinking about him." Juan stared around the room, and added in a low voice, "I don't want to die, Concepción. Not ever."

"But death—" she began, and stopped. "Death —that is a natural part of life, Juan. It is sweet and simple and—"

Juan got to his feet. "What do you know about it?" he said ill-humoredly, and shivered. Concepción always said that, but since she, her own self, had never personally died, he didn't see how to believe her.

Juan's prayers at night were brief. He wished long life and happiness for himself, for Concepción, for his mother and father, and when he remembered, for Emilio. He usually added Luiscito because he shared the mattress and Juan didn't want him to die there before morning. But he did not go on to the rest of them, the sisters, or Sister Angela, or the other orphans or the Cura. It wasn't that he didn't like the others, except the Cura. It was that he used up all his passionate wishfulness on himself and Concepción. It was the best he could do.

As for Father Antonio—well, Juan didn't dare wish him dead, but if he could have prayed him into another town, or another country, or another world, and not get found out, he would not have hesitated a moment.

Sometimes he didn't know what he wanted most. A party in the fields, a pair of red rubber boots, or to wake up one morning to find the Cura had disappeared in the night and who cared how.

chapter

six

"Come on," said Concepción. "We're going to the Bean Bank."

"O*kay!*" said Juan, thoughts of Pablo, death, and the Cura falling from his mind at the thrust of this wonderful news.

"Sister Angela says we can get the rice. And Emilio can come too, if he wants."

"Hey, Emilio!" shouted Juan from the doorway. "Emilio!"

Emilio, who had dropped out of the soccer game, came trotting over.

"We're going to the Bean Bank!" Juan shouted at him happily, and Emilio's homely face lighted up with joy.

The square was four blocks from Casa María, and Juan and Emilio raced off, leaving Concepción to follow. They had time to run twice around the plaza before she appeared, and they ran up to her laughing, pulling her down on a bench.

"Let's not go right away, to the Bean Bank," said Juan.

"Let's sit here and look at the people," Emilio begged. "Let's look at the clouds and see things in them, Concepción."

The three of them looked up, studying the broad heavens, where a few clouds moved slowly, lazily changing shape as they traversed the sky.

"See, that's an iguana," said Emilio, pointing. "See its legs, and its mouth opening to eat the little cloud in front?"

"No," said Concepción. "The little cloud is in back. It's a little boat, attached to a big boat that is sailing away. We could get on it," she continued in a dreamlike voice, "and sail away, too."

"Where would we go, Concepción?" asked Juan, as he and Emilio wriggled happily, thinking what it would be like to be on that boat like a cloud. Or, thought Juan, on a cloud like a bus, like the one in the dormitory. Or on a cloud like an airplane. Or on anything that moved and went—far away.

30

"Anywhere," Concepción said, sighing. "Just away."

"Far far away," said Emilio.

But they smiled because, for a little while, they were away.

The square, at this hour, was filled with people, some of them sunning on the benches like themselves, some sleeping. Others moved as if with purpose, into the bank, the *parroquia,* the supermarket. Nobody hurried, except a small burro, his back piled high with kindling, who dashed down the street, his master flicking at his rump with a twig. There were all sorts of shops. A tinsmith's, a carpenter's. Shops that sold embroidery and bright painted animals for the tourists to buy. There was the police station, and a bakery. A bar, where men sat around a table playing cards. Others threw dice. And all, Juan guessed, drank tequila. There was a radio in the bar that blared all over the square. Mariachi music, loud and lively, rending the air.

A couple of tourists came out of the hotel on the corner and stood a moment, looking around with smiles of pleasure.

Juan looked at them curiously. A nice tall tubby man in the fancy clothes that *norteamericanos* wore. A flowered shirt, bright green pants. The lady with him had hair the color of ripe mangoes and a short pink dress. Juan found her beautiful, beautiful.

I wish them to walk over here, he said to himself. I want them somehow to come over here where we are, and see us.

He did not pose this as a prayer, because Father Antonio had warned them about praying for "trivial" things. If you prayed for just anything you wanted, by the time you got around to praying for eternal life, you'd have used up your share, said the Cura. At least, it seemed to Juan that was what he said. With the Cura, often you couldn't be sure.

Come here! Come this way! he implored the tourist couple, who looked this way and that and then started across the square.

They stopped for a moment to smile at a couple of children playing pony. One boy had a string between his teeth, and the other held it like reins as they galloped around, the pony snorting, the rider yelling.

Now, why couldn't Emilio and I have been doing that? thought Juan, desperately feeling in his pockets for some string that he knew wasn't there. Why couldn't we be doing *something* that would make them stop and smile?

The tall couple continued on, staring here and there with delight. They stopped again, the lady clutching the man's arm, pointing up at the *parroquia*.

"It's glorious!" she said, and now they were close enough so that Juan could hear her. Though he knew a little American, he didn't understand what she was saying in her clear voice. "It's so ornate, so—so human and warm, isn't it? Isn't it?"

The man tipped his straw hat back and stared upward at the big church. He studied its lacy façade. Juan turned to look at it, too. There were pigeons roosting on all the spires, flying in and out of the bell towers. It looked rosy and warm in the sunlight, this *parroquia* that he had never much noticed before, though he and all the other children went there to mass at six o'clock every morning.

"It's a dandy, all right," said the man. He glanced toward the bar, shaking his head, grinning. "They certainly like their music loud."

"They want to hear it," she agreed, and they came on.

"Complaining because the music is too loud," Concepción said scornfully. "Who's making them listen?"

"They couldn't *not* listen," said Juan. Suddenly he was on his feet, confronting the tourists. "It's the mariachis, Señor, Mister," he said, looking full into the man's face. He didn't dare address the Señora, thinking it might be impolite. But it was all right for a boy to talk to a man.

He heard Concepción's gasp of surprise, and Emilio's giggle, but ignored them.

"The mariachis, Señor. Very fine music-makers." He was trying to speak in American, having learned some from Concepción, who had learned to speak it very well from Sister Angela.

Now he transferred his gaze to the woman, to find her looking down at him with the—the most beautiful expression he had ever seen. It was the sort of look that Concepción often gave him, except that Concepción did not have so lovely a face.

"How do you do, *muchacho*," she said in Spanish.

Juan's smile widened as he said he did well and hoped fervently that she did the same. "You know Spanish, Señora."

She laughed. "A little. But I am taking lessons at home so that some day I can come back and talk like a native."

"But you talk very good, Señora," he told her eagerly. He heard Concepción sniff. It was true, the lady's accent was not perfection, but Juan lifted his voice and repeated, "*Very* good."

"And you—you're learning to speak English, I see."

"American," he said. "I learn American."

She laughed again, and put a light hand on his shoulder. "What is your name, little one?"

"Juan."

"And where do you live?"

Concepción was on her feet, holding her rebozo close around her. "We live at the Casa María, Señora. The orphanage. Come Juan, Emilio. We must go."

"But I'm not an—"Juan began wildly, only to find he was talking to the tourists' backs.

The Señora looked over her shoulder and said, "*Adiós, Juan*. See you again."

But the man was saying, "Don't you see the girl doesn't want us talking to them? Don't upset her. Now come on."

Juan didn't understand all of what he said, but enough to judge that everything was Concepción's fault.

"Why did you do that?" he said angrily. "We were having—we were having a nice *talk*. Why did you spoil it, Concepción?"

"I'm sorry." Her face was bitter and sad. "I—we do have to hurry, Juan. We should get the rice and return to Casa María. Sister Angela won't let us out again if we stay away too long. You know that."

"Yes," Emilio agreed, urging them along by increasing his walk to a trot. "You want to spoil it for *us*, Juan?"

Juan trudged behind them, lingered outside while Concepción got the two bags of rice at the Bean Bank. Usually he liked to go in and see all the neat and beautiful bins of beans arranged according to kind. Black, ivory, brown with red eyes. Señor Sautello, who kept the Bean Bank, so called because he both sold beans and had a little bank where he kept money for the towns-people and the cowboys who worked on the ranches, handed two bags of rice to Concepción. He talked to her and Emilio for a moment, and then they hurried out.

On the way back, Concepción said abruptly, "She was pretty, that *gringa*, wasn't she?"

Juan looked at Concepción's smooth face with its dark shining eyes now blinking with tears.

He wanted to say, "You're pretty, too, Con-cepción." But she had rushed ahead, and any-way, he couldn't say something like that in front of Emilio.

chapter

seven

"Can I help you find something?" Concepción asked the next morning, stopping at the door of the boys' dormitory.

"If you know what I'm looking for," said Juan. Concepción laughed. "Suppose you tell me."

"Well, it's my frog."

"*Your* frog?"

"Yes, my frog."

Juan sat back on his heels. He'd searched under all the mattresses lying against the wall, and under the tiers of triple-deck bunks, and along the shelves where the children kept their clothes.

"Yesterday afternoon," Juan explained, "at the playground, I found this tiny frog. He followed me, you see, so I put him in my pocket."

"I see," said Concepción.

"And last night I put him back there"—he gestured with a thin brown hand—"in that corner. Where he'd be safe. And when I looked for him this morning, there he was—gone."

"Did you want him for a pet?" Concepción said tenderly.

Juan ducked his head, looking up at her slantwise.

"Juan," she said, tenderness replaced at once by suspicion, "Juan, what were your plans for that frog?"

"What do you care?"

"Well, I do care."

"Why?"

"I care about everything about you."

This was irresistible and Juan bit his lip, wavering between a lie, a half-lie, or, just possibly, the truth.

"The truth, Juan," said Concepción as he debated.

How she always figured out what he was thinking, Juan could not tell. But if she hadn't, if sometimes he'd been able to fool her, he would not have liked it.

He was able to deceive and lie to just about everybody else. Sister Angela could often tell his real lies, but she had trouble with his half-lies. Father Antonio knew when he was lying but not when he was telling the truth. Only Concepción knew him, and even at his wiliest he relied on her to go on knowing him.

This time he decided on the truth, since he knew it would either annoy or sadden her. Juan found that next to having her love him, he most liked to make Concepción angry or sad. He guessed he was a wicked boy. The Cura certainly thought so, and told him often enough, and the Cura couldn't be wrong about everything.

"I was going to put a spell on it, on my frog, and get it to hop to Father Antonio's house and sit on his forehead when he's sleeping and draw out all his thinking so when he wakes up he won't be able to think or talk or anything."

"Juan!"

Juan lifted his shoulders. "Frog's gone, anyhow. Unless I could maybe find another one."

"Juan, *will* you stop talking this way? It's wicked, that's what it is. Besides, you know you don't know how to make spells, or make frogs hop where you want them to, and you can't fix it for a frog to draw out a person's thinking. Now, I want you to take back such awful talk."

"My grandfather was a medicine man," said Juan with assurance.

"He was?" said Concepción. And then, "Oh, Juan. Really. How can you know who your grandfather was when you—you aren't sure who your parents were—are?"

"I know because he comes to me when I'm dreaming and he tells me all sorts of stuff. Like how to put a spell on a frog," Juan said craftily.

Concepción thought for a moment she was just going to walk off and leave him with his bad stupid plans that would in no case work out, grandfather or no grandfather. But she looked into his lustrous eyes, turned up to hers, and put her arms around him.

"Why do you think such things? Why do you hate Father Antonio? He's not a bad man. What's the matter with you, Little Turtle?"

"He is a bad man. He hates me."

"No."

"Yes. And he tells me I'm wicked and mischievous and a liar."

"But you are a—well, you do tell untruths."

Concepción saw his lips tighten, and thought to herself that sometimes her Little Turtle seemed to be a snapping turtle.

"And he says I'm an orphan."

Concepción put her arms around him, but he pulled away.

"You think I'm one, too."

"No."

"Do you think I'm not?"

"Oh, Juan, Juan. I don't know. How can I

know? I'm just a girl. I only know—I love you, Juan."

He stood looking up at her coldly, although a spark inside him glowed at the words. Concepción didn't often use the word *love*. Juan never did. He was saving it for his parents. So now, even though the look on her face was so lonely, so sorrowful, that he wanted to reach up and pat her cheek gently, he continued to stare at her without warmth.

He was the only one in the whole world who believed in his parents.

"Juan," she was saying, "why have you started spending all your time in here? Why don't you go out and play soccer with the others?"

"I don't want to."

"But why not?"

"Concepción, I don't *know* why. The courtyard is dark."

"It's dark in here."

"But I'm not supposed to be playing soccer in here. Why can't we ever go anywhere nice to play? Concepción, let's run away and live in a tent in the fields. We can take Emilio."

She decided he was joking, so she laughed very hard. "What a crazy idea, Juan. Where do you *get* such notions?"

Juan wanted to cry, so he shouted at her to leave him alone, and, after all, ran out to join

42

in the game. He was a hard and driving player, better than boys much older than he, and today he outdid himself, always remembering to send a lazy, easy ball, now and then, to Emilio.

When the bell rang for classes, he was in a fine mood and couldn't understand what was wrong with Concepción, who came out of the kitchen where she worked mornings, her mouth drooping, her eyes misty.

He gave her an impatient glance. Why couldn't she be cheery and bright, the way he was?

"Concepción," he said angrily. "What's the matter with you? Why can't you be merry?"

Concepción gave him a look of reproach, that altered to one of irritation, that gave way to one of amusement.

She shook her head. "Snapping Turtle," she murmured and moved down the hall, her thin little figure moving lightly.

chapter
eight

"What would you do if you could do anything you wanted to? If anybody would let you." asked Emilio as the children trudged in double file back to Casa María. They had been to the *parroquia* to confess and receive communion.

"Run away," said Juan.

"No, but I mean really."

"So do I mean really. I'd run away."

"Where to?"

Juan considered. "I guess Mexico City. Anyway, I'd start from there."

"How would you get there?"

"Walk."

"It's awfully far. Maybe a hundred miles. Maybe a thousand miles," said Emilio, stumbling over a cobblestone and almost going to his knees.

"If you keep walking long enough, you could walk around the world," said Juan, paying no attention, since Emilio stumbled much of the time.

"How about the ocean? Are you going to walk on the water, like Our Lord?"

"Maybe."

Emilio didn't think that was reverent. "You better not let Father Antonio hear you say that."

Juan shrugged. "You could get on a boat and keep walking around and around it," he said. "That way you could walk around the world."

"They'd catch you."

Juan wasn't sure about that. From time to time children disappeared from Casa María and weren't brought back. Juan thought maybe he'd looked for his frog harder than Father Antonio and "The Board" would look for a runaway orphan. He decided not to mention this to Emilio, who'd then ask why didn't he just start running.

Someday, Juan told himself. Someday. When he was older. Then, maybe. Or if Concepción left the orphanage and got a job in the hotel, like Adela, or ran off with a cowboy, the way another girl had. Then he'd leave Casa María for good.

But the truth was—the truth was—

Well, not exactly the truth, because he wasn't exactly afraid. What it is, is, he assured himself, is that I have to wait here to see if my parents find me. Then, if they don't—if they don't find me by the time I'm ten—then I'll run away to Mexico City and get a job as a shoeshine boy.

He had heard, from people here and there, that boys in Mexico City made big moneys shining shoes for *gringos* and rich Mexicans. All you needed was a box, some polish, a rag and a way about you. That was what Adela had said. Juan figured there'd have to be some way to get the box, the polish and the rag. As to "a way about you," Juan wasn't sure what it meant but suspected he could manage that, too.

The people would pay you for the shoeshine, and then give you extra, too. Tips. With enough of those tips, he could—well, he could do a lot of things.

"What would you do," he asked Emilio, "if you had a lot of money?"

"Buy candy."

They sighed.

"What would you do?" Emilio asked, though he knew the answer.

"Get a pair of red rubber boots," said Juan, not disappointing him.

Juan had been wanting a pair of red rubber boots for months. Ever since the day last summer when they'd been coming back from the playground and a storm had come up, swiftly and suddenly the way storms did in July.

He'd been running toward Casa María with his head down when he'd spied, running in the opposite direction, a pair of gleaming, shining, twinkling, bright red rubber boots. He'd stopped still, staring after them, shivering with cold, with wet, with envy. They'd been on the feet of a *norteamericano*, a boy about his own age, but Juan had scarcely noticed the boy. He'd seen, like a vision, his own self running in the rain with those shining boots going boldly through puddles, feet safe and cozy inside the glory of the boots.

Oh, how he would splash through the deepest and widest puddles the rain could make! How he would love the rain and never care if the sun came out again, if he had such a pair of boots!

Emilio, who had missed the glorious sight that day, had heard enough about the boots since then to feel he'd actually seen them. For his own part, what money he ever had, though he didn't expect to have any, would go for candy.

But he knew how Juan felt, wanting something so much. Emilio, of course, had a personal possession. He had a picture of his parents in what was said to be a solid gold frame. It was one of the great treasures of Casa María, besides the three-quarter violin that Fortuno had brought to the orphanage with him, a gift from his uncle, and the pink taffeta shawl Adela had kept in a box and worn on fiesta days even though Sister Angela and the Cura said it showed selfishness and vanity.

These valuable things, except the shawl, which Adela had taken with her when she left to work in the hotel, were housed in a cupboard for safekeeping. Even Emilio's parents' picture was there now. For a long time he had kept it on the shelf above his mattress, but had accidentally knocked it off and broken the glass, so Sister Angela said it would be safer in the cupboard. Still, he could look at it whenever he wanted to. And he knew it was there, something of his own. Juan had nothing.

Juan said, "Is there going to be that party, Emilio, do you think? That party somebody said somebody was going to give us, up in the fields?"

Emilio sparkled. "You think so, Juan? You really think so?"

"I was asking you," Juan snapped. He'd wanted Emilio to say yes, of course there'd be a party, but Emilio was this careful sort who only said what he was sure of.

Juan gave him a look of contempt, and then suddenly, without warning, without even knowing a second in advance that he was going to do it, Juan turned and sped off.

chapter
nine

He didn't stop to think what he was doing, where he was going, what was going to happen to him because he did this wild thing. He simply ran.

Down the cobbled street that led toward town he flew at soccer speed. He heard, or perhaps just felt, Emilio call after him. He felt the startled eyes of the other children in the line, staring after his running figure. He dodged around a corner and kept racing away from the double file of orphans on their way to the orphanage.

Away from Emilio and Luiscito and Esteban and Fortuno. Away from Concepción.

At this, he stopped, breathless, and leaned against a wall to think.

Concepción.

What would she do when she found him gone? Cry? Get angry? Put on her shawl and come looking for him? Yes, that's what she would do. Look for him. So he must be very careful not to be found. Because now that he had run, there'd be no going back.

Probably Father Antonio wouldn't let him back in Casa María if he wanted to be let in, and he'd never want to be.

But Concepción would hunt until she found him, and then she'd be after everybody—Sister Angela, the Cura, that group of ladies who were very grand and were called "The Board," and came once a month to look at the children and pretend to smile at them—Concepción would keep after them all until somebody gave in and said, "Yes, yes, let him return. *If*—he promises to be good all the rest of his life, never to lie again or laugh or make a mistake, always to remember what a bad boy he was and confess it every day and repent and pray to be made better."

Well, said Juan to himself, I certainly can't do that. Things had been awful enough at Casa María before. After this, he'd be miserable every day of his life, and if he forgot, someone would remind him.

He moved away from the wall and walked

thoughtfully across the square. It all looked as it had the day he and Concepción and Emilio had come here on their way to the Bean Bank.

Remembering how happy he'd been that day— or anyway, until Concepción got jealous of the American lady—he felt his heart actually sort of squeeze with pain. Because he *had* been happy that day. And other days, too. He'd been happy, sometimes, at Casa María, and he wondered now how it was he hadn't known it.

Sitting on a bench, nervously, like a bird perching only long enough to decide which way to fly, he glanced at an old man at the other end.

Probably, he decided, that old man will look around at me in a few minutes and say, "What are you doing here, young fellow?" And I'll say, "I've run away." "Where from?" he'll ask me, and after a little bit, I'll tell him. "From Casa María," I'll say. Because that's what I have to say. And then he'll say, "Well, we'll just have to see about that, won't we? Can't have young fellows running away like that, sets a bad example." And then he will take me home. I mean, back to Casa María. He'll *make* me go. That wouldn't be like going back on my own. That would be being *brought* back, forced to return by an old man. I couldn't disobey an old man.

So it was just a matter of waiting until he was found out by—he glanced hopefully down the bench, but the old man had tipped his sombrero over his eyes and was snoring.

Juan gave a little gasping sound, close to a sob. But the old man went on snoring. And nobody else in the whole square was paying any attention to him.

He sat for quite a while, looking longingly at the hotel where he'd seen the American couple come out the other day. If only they'd come out again now. Walk out on the street with those handsome, happy, gold-skinned faces and walk into the square, and see him.

"Why, Juan"—the lady would say, remembering him immediately—"why, Juan—what are you doing here?"

And he'd explain, and they'd take him home. Or, maybe—maybe they'd take him with them. He'd go back with them to the U. S. of A. and never see this town or anyone in it again.

He sighed, hunched his shoulders a little, telling himself that they had probably been gone for days. In their car. Or in one of those big buses that came into the square and then took off again to exciting places. Bit towns like Celaya or Guadalajara. Or even Mexico City.

They weren't going to come out of the hotel and find him.

And Concepción. Where was she? Was she just going to let him run away, let him go, and not come looking for him at all?

In front of the police station, two policemen stood at attention, holding guns and looking mean enough to use them on a runaway boy.

Watching those two, Juan decided he'd better get out of the square. He turned a corner, walked past a drugstore and a woodworking shop, turned another corner and arrived at the market.

All at once, he felt fine.

A smile darting at his lips, he surveyed this marvelous scene.

All the stalls, set so close together, selling such beautiful things under their sagging canvas roofs. Great mounds of oranges and mangoes and little hard green limes. Thin cucumbers, petal-like lettuce heads, clusters of small dark bananas. Flower stalls, piled and heaped with daisies and snapdragons and roses and lilies, and other stalls with paper flowers, bigger and fancier by far than real ones.

Stalls with beads and buttons and scissors and ribbons and rebozos and little tiny statues of the Virgin and Our Lord.

Forgetful of himself, of Casa María, of Concepción, Juan wandered in his freedom, taking deep breaths of the air that was flowery and greasy at once.

Some of the merchants didn't have stalls. They had patches of space where they squatted, their wares beside them. One old woman had neat little piles of piñon nuts, beans, and slices of orange-colored squash. You could hardly see her inside her dark clothes, the rebozo over her head and dropping over her face. She kept shooing away chickens who wandered about the market pecking anxiously through the refuse.

Now a young cock came down the cobbles with a hesitating strut. He would advance a step, poise with his foot in the air, press it carefully to the ground, advance another step, all the while looking keenly about him. When he'd progressed a certain distance, he would stop, lift his head and thrust it forward, and crow.

Juan watched him with pleasure. He liked the way the bronze and black and green feathers glinted in the sun, the way the fountain of his tail swung idly, the way he crowed, so loud and sure of himself, and then tipped his head to listen for answering crows.

The sound of cocks crowing was a part of this town, like the sound of bells, and birds, and burros braying, and mariachi music bursting out of windows from radios everywhere.

Juan adored the noise. He loved the smells and pushing and crowding of the marketplace.

For a while he stopped to watch a machine that turned out such layers and layers of tortillas that you'd think all of the town could never

consume them. Juan's mouth watered as he looked, and he moved on, just beginning to wonder what he'd do when he got hungry.

He was hungry already, but that was just the usual way he felt. All the children in Casa María felt hungry most of the time. Emilio said it was because they didn't get enough candy, but Juan wasn't sure of that. They got lots of rice and beans, though, so maybe Emilio was right. Maybe it was just always wanting something sweet that made you feel hungry even if you'd just eaten a plate of rice and beans.

But what if you couldn't get rice and beans?

Juan licked his upper lip and considered the situation. Now he was hungry, but that was okay, that didn't bother him. What about later, when he was starving? Tonight, about suppertime, he'd begin to think about them all sitting at the long wooden tables, eating rice and beans from their tin plates, drinking milk from their tin mugs. What would happen then? What would he do? Sneak back and try to get in and pretend it had all been a mistake? Swear he hadn't run away, that he had got lost by accident, or waylaid by bandits?

But they had all *seen* him run away.

He walked on, more slowly, not looking around with quite so much interest.

And yet—and yet—

It was a fine feeling, to be free, to be saunter-ing in the market, in the sunshine, with no one to tell him what to do or where to go. He could decide those things for himself. He could sit down now, if he wanted to, and just watch the people.

The cowboys, in from the ranches, moving down the middle of the streets as if they owned them, wearing their bright and beaded vests and their big sombreros and their cocky smirky smiles. The old women, hobbling, all in black, putting out their claw-hands for tourists to drop centavos in. The tourists, big and clean and out-dressing the cowboys. Once again Juan looked for his own two tourists, especially the lady, but without any hope.

He sat on a bench and watched and nobody looked at him.

But *nobody* looks at me, he said to himself. Not the tourists or the cowboys or other children going by. He was just another boy, and the town was full of boys. He wasn't somebody that any-body would bother to look at. Except Concep-ción.

Young or old, tourist or Mexican, all the peo-ple passed and didn't seem to know that he was sitting on a bench here, free, and getting very hungry.

chapter

ten

He got up and walked on. There were stalls now where clothes were sold. Dresses and shawls and pants and leather vests and different sorts of hats. He stopped. There was a booth with about a thousand pair of shoes and sandals —and boots.

He moved closer.

They hung high on a hook. A pair of gleaming red rubber boots. They started out like an explosion from the black and brown boots around them, and they swayed a little as the stallkeeper stood up to remove a pair of fancy tooled sandals next to them.

Juan looked at the boots as he'd looked at the tortillas, with the same ache in his stomach.

His mouth began to water in just the same way. And then, as he'd left the tortillas behind because he wanted them so much and couldn't have them, he moved away from the stall with the boots.

Just about my size, he thought. Those boots. Somebody would buy them for a boy just about his size, to wear in the rain, through puddles, as much as he wanted to.

"*Ay,*" said Juan to himself. *I-eee*, it rang in his head.

His foot nudged something soft and he stared down, then quickly looked around. Still nobody was watching him. He stooped, snatched up the two little bananas that had fallen there somehow, who knew how, and walked quickly around a corner so that the owner of the bananas, if he should come back looking, would not see who'd got them.

When he was far enough away, he judged, so that no one could identify these particular two bananas, he found another bench and sat down to eat, slowly, with great deliberation, savoring them. They were ripe and sweet and warm and never in his life before had he tasted anything quite so good.

After a while he dropped the peels on the ground, and sighed and stood up and began wandering again.

It was a funny thing, this freedom. He could do anything. Unless it cost money. He could go anywhere. He could start walking to Mexico City if he wanted to, and nobody would stop him. So why couldn't he think of anything to do?

He wasn't going to walk to Mexico City. Not yet, not today. It was too far to go for someone who had only eaten two bananas since morning, and those by mistake. He wouldn't find any more. He might start for Mexico City tomorrow, but it was too late today. He'd been through the market many times. He was afraid to go to the square, because of those policemen, and because Concepción might find him there. The square was where she would look for him.

So he walked on, and found himself back in the very center of the square, the plaza where a little bandstand stood, and there were benches all around where the people were sitting, reading or talking or dozing in the late afternoon sun. Some boys were shining tourists' shoes, and pocketing money.

I wonder if I could steal a shoeshine box, Juan said to himself. But he knew he couldn't. Those boys, most of them no older than himself and a couple younger, appeared tough enough to kill you if you took their box.

He sat down on another bench and tried to figure out if it was the fifth or sixth he'd sat on so far. Freedom was a funny thing if it came out to just going from one bench to another all day long, looking at people but never being looked at. He was used to attention. Even if it wasn't always the sort of attention he wanted, at Casa María he got it.

At Casa María just now—he looked at the great clock in the *parroquia* to check the time, which he was able to do because Concepción had taught him—at Casa María just now they'd be sitting down to supper. Afterwards they'd go out in the courtyard and knock the ball around. And in a while they'd go to bed, and Emilio and Luiscito would have the whole entire mattress to themselves tonight. Juan's lower lip stuck out as he thought about all this.

They'll miss me, I guess, he said to himself. They will be jealous, too. Because I'm free and gone forever and they're still there. And Concepción will miss me.

He began to breathe harder, thinking about Concepción, and about how here he was, right in the square, and she didn't come and didn't come. He'd thought, when he first came to the square, to find her rushing about, her eyes racing from boy to boy all over the place until at last she found him and let fly with angry words. Oh, the things Concepción would think of to say when she found him!

But she hadn't found him. She hadn't come at all.

He'd been here and *been* here. It must be close to three hours now, sitting here in the plaza, waiting to be discovered, and the dark was coming and even the shoeshine boys were gone somewhere—to their homes, probably, where their mothers would give them something to eat and tell them what smart boys they were.

Here he was, and Concepción didn't bother to come at all.

His anger at her throbbed in his head, and he could feel his blood pumping inside him. All her talk and her sighs and her eyes and calling him Little Turtle and saying she loved him and then when he was gone—*she didn't even bother to find him.*

When he did see her, coming around the corner from the street leading down from Casa María, her eyes red and teary and staring, her hands holding each other the way they did when she was unhappy, Juan was so beside himself with pain and rage that he slipped away in the gathering dark to leave her wandering in search of him.

Let her be unhappy, he said to himself in a small hard voice. Let her be so unhappy that she—she—

Let her look and look and look and not find

him and cry for months and never feel better and—

He stopped running and looked around, shivering with hunger, with anger, with loneliness. Where was he now? He didn't know. There was a sort of dump yard to one side. A row of low, tacked-together houses on the other. Some chickens and goats scratched around in the dust, and through rents in the tattered curtains hanging at doorways he could see families at tables with one or two candles burning.

But it was night, and these candles didn't touch the darkness. Juan felt the tears start down his face, and he didn't even bother to stop crying.

Next to one of the houses was a shed, and he crept into it, so he could cry in peace and not out there where someone might see him. There was a pig in the shed. A nice bristly smelly pig that grunted when he came in and then seemed to move over and make a place for him.

Juan lay down, close to the pig, and cried himself to sleep.

chapter
eleven

At dawn the pig started, snorted, staggered to its feet snarling in a manner that sent Juan flying from the shed and up the street. He couldn't figure out why the pig had let him sleep there so snugly all night and then at the first light had looked and plainly hated him.

Unless, he said to himself, last night he thought I was another pig. It was not an entirely pleasing idea and Juan was scowling about it when he bumped into the Cura.

All at once two big hands were roughly shaking him by the shoulders and a voice as angry as the pig's was in his ears.

"What do you think you're doing, you little mischief-maker? What made you do such a thing that has Sister Angela and Concepción, who've been so good to you, weeping and praying all night, and half the town out looking for you? Answer me, you person!"

Juan, who didn't believe that anyone but Concepción had looked for him, tried to stare insolently in Father Antonio's eyes. But, unnerved by hunger, by uncertainty about what was going to happen to him now, and not least by the pig's unexpected hostility, he began to cry instead. He bawled loudly as Father Antonio dragged him through the streets back toward Casa María.

And, he thought bitterly, people were staring at him today, all right. Yesterday he was invisible. This morning it seemed everyone everywhere was looking at him and laughing.

But he couldn't stop howling and sniveling. Humiliated, famished, hurt by the Cura's rough grasp, and terrified of what lay ahead, he was pulled through the streets in an uproar. Only as they got near the orphanage did he start to assemble himself, rub his eyes and nose with his sleeve, gulp down some remaining sobs, and straighten, so as to look his own man.

As they rounded the corner of the street of Casa María, the Cura's grip on him slackened, and for one moment, one brief, rebellious, heartening moment, Juan thought to run again. He

flicked a quick glance up at Father Antonio's face and found the grey eyes fixed on his with a look of knowing.

"Go ahead," said Father Antonio. "Run. I don't know what to, and next time I won't collar you and bring you back. Next time, I might not even let you in. But run, run . . . if you want to."

Juan shivered with hatred and let himself be conducted back in through the doors of the orphanage, into the dining room where all the children, seated at the long wooden tables, looked up wordlessly.

Concepción half-started from her seat, then sank back again. Sister Angela's face grew smooth with sadness and reproach, but she just murmured, "Sit down, Juan. Eat your breakfast."

Juan moved his shoulders back, swaggered to his place between Emilio and Fortuno, and made himself lift a spoonful of hot cereal slowly, as if he couldn't care less, to his mouth. But he closed his eyes briefly at the bliss of having food to taste, to swallow, once again, and when he opened them, he looked directly into Concepción's eyes and winked at her.

After breakfast, Concepción began clearing the table without even looking at Juan, and when he came to stand beside her, she walked away toward the kitchen with a trayful of dishes, not looking back.

Juan stared after her thoughtfully, piling plates ready for her next trip.

"Don't be angry," he said when she returned, tight-lipped and silent. "Concepción," he coaxed, "don't hate me."

Still she didn't talk. She piled dishes without a word and turned, without a word, away.

"All right," Juan called after her. "All right, Concepción. You hate me, too. The Cura does, and the pig does, and I guess everybody does so you can too, and what do I care. I don't care about any of you, see? And I'll run away again and this time I won't come back. Concepción!"

Then she put the tray down and turned to him, her arms open so he could come into them and stand against her, weak and tired from the strain of all these long hours.

Sometimes Concepción surprised him by not saying what he would expect grown people—and Concepción was practically grown up—to say. Now she didn't ask him anything. Not why he'd done it, not did he know how unhappy he'd made her, made other people. Nothing. She just held him close for a moment and then said he could help her with the clearing up.

But later in the day she said, "You know, Juan, Father Antonio *did* bring you home."

Silence from Juan.

"He could have just forgotten about you. But he looked for you."

"He didn't look. I ran into him."

"We all looked," Concepción said, and Juan believed her.

chapter
twelve

It was Saturday, and there was no school. On Saturdays, in the morning after breakfast, came cleanup time. The children, including the boys, with buckets and rags and brooms, cleaned out the dormitories, the dining room, the classrooms, the chapel.

The big girls cleaned the parlor where "The Board" met once a month. It was the sunniest room in the building and had nice furniture in it. Most of the children never saw it and none of them ever went in except the girls assigned to clean it. The big girls also took the orphanage laundry to outdoor public tubs where they soaped and pounded and rinsed the clothes and then carried it all back to hang on lines in the sunless courtyard.

When the cleanup was finished, the children, barred from the laundry-hung courtyard, were taken to the playground.

Although he'd kept expecting to be called to Father Antonio's presence, or at least to Sister Angela's, to be told how bad he was and to be punished, the morning went on with no word for Juan. He accompanied the others to the playground, where he appropriated a swing for himself and swung up and down, thinking about how brave he'd been, how he'd endured hunger and loneliness and that attack from what had maybe been a wild boar that had accidentally got in the shed, as he himself had accidentally got in it.

"Don't you want to play soccer?" asked Emilio, coming over to stand beside the swing.

"No."

"Oh."

When Emilio said nothing more but just stood there waiting, Juan let the swing creak to a stop.

"Where did you go?" Emilio asked.

Juan lifted his shoulders. "Where I wanted to. Anywhere. To the market."

"Hey-hey," said Emilio enviously, and added, "I bet you were awfully hungry. I bet you were starved."

"Why should I be? People gave me things to eat. A lady making tortillas gave me all I wanted, and somebody else gave me two bananas, and somebody else gave me candy and cake—"

Carried away, he realized too late that Emilio was looking at him with doubt. I always *say* too much, Juan told himself irritably. I never stop in time not to sound like a liar. He was convinced that there was some trick in lying, if he could only learn. Some way to do it so that people believed you.

"Anyway, I did find some bananas," he said. "And Emilio—in the market, in a booth where they sell shoes and things, there's a pair of—"

Emilio interrupted loudly, "Juan, don't start talking about red rubber boots again. Everybody's tired of hearing about them. I want to know what you *did*. I mean, besides going to the market. You were out *all night*," he said in a tone of wonder that reestablished Juan's confidence in himself. "I mean, Juan—did you get to see the fireworks?"

Juan looked blank. Fireworks? Then, as if hearing it for the first time, he recalled the fierce and bursting sound of fireworks crowding the air as he sobbed against the pig's bristly back in the dark. And there'd been the sound of a band, too. There had been a fiesta of some sort in the square last night and he must have fallen asleep without really noticing.

"Well, sure I saw them," he said. "What do you think? I sat on a bench in the square and listened to the band play, and watched the fireworks—"

The scene gleamed in his mind and so was transmitted to Emilio.

The great wooden frame of fireworks loomed in front of the *parroquia*, waiting to be touched off. The band was dressed in white trousers and blue jackets with gold braid pressed all over them, playing fine and military music. The mariachis in their fringed vests and enormous sombreros strolled and sang and shook the air with their music when the band had finished. And around and around the square the people paraded, girls going one way and boys another.

As he told Emilio about it, Juan began to be conscious of having known all this before, as if he had truly been in the square, in all the excitement of fiesta night. Maybe I walked in my sleep, he said to himself. Because he saw and heard the band, saw the laughing girls and boys circling and circling, looking at each other the way older boys and girls did. He saw the mariachis with their guitars slung round their shoulders and their mustaches flaring. He felt the breathless moment when the torch was applied to the wooden fireworks frame and the night exploded into great stars and fountains and flowers,

75

of colored light. There were Roman candles, and whirling *castillo de fuego* and waterfalls of silver light, and the people cheering . . .

". . . everything bursting and booming and popping," he told the gaping Emilio. "I never saw anything like it," he said, and frowned a little. Because he never *had*, last night or any other time, seen anything like it, had he? Or had he?

And then, in his mind, in his memory, he knew how he could tell all this as if he had been there.

Pablo. Pablo Ortiz had told him this very story, the way he was telling it now to Emilio. A couple of years ago, when Pablo had slipped out of Casa María one evening, to go to a fiesta, to see what it was like, he had described it all this way.

Pablo had got back into the orphanage without being caught or found out. Or—Juan asked himself pensively—or was it that Pablo had never actually got out? Had Pablo, too, made things up, perhaps from something somebody *else* had made up, and made it all so real that he believed in it himself, as Juan frequently believed in his own stories?

It made him feel comfortable, to think of all those people telling things that weren't true.

Besides, what could he do? Tell Emilio that he'd spent his night of freedom in a shed with a pig? That he'd been bawling so loud and then had fallen asleep so hard that he hadn't even noticed a fiesta was taking place?

What fun would that be for Emilio?

"That was when the lady gave me the cake and candy," he said. "During the fireworks."

This time Emilio nodded acceptance.

Juan had discovered that sometimes if people didn't believe your lie the first time, if you repeated it a little later, then they did. He supposed vaguely that it was because most people didn't lie at all, and so wouldn't think somebody would try the same one twice.

How funny it is, he said to himself. How funny the whole entire world is, he thought, as he and Emilio shared a happy and highly colored untruth.

chapter
thirteen

That evening, in the chapel, the children sat after prayers waiting for Father Antonio, who was to come and tell them something.

All afternoon the rumor, riper now than ever, had been flying through the orphanage, from child to child, setting them rustling and whispering together. Juan had questioned Concepción closely about it, but she didn't know, and they'd ended just by talking about the other times.

But now all the children sat together in tense silence, biting their lips, glancing at one another. Hoping.

Juan looked over at the girls' side, where Concepción was kneeling, her hands together, pressed against her bowed head.

Praying for a party? Juan thought. And then, No, praying for me. Concepción prayed for him every day, and at night before she went to sleep. Juan knew because she'd told him so. She prayed that he'd be happy and healthy and good and grow up wise and kind and perfect.

Juan thought it was nice of her to do this, although he had very little hope that her prayers would be answered. Except he was healthy.

He looked at the bowed heads of the children around him and thought, all at once, and for the first time that he could remember, that he was, in a way, happy. Not happy, he knew, like people who had parents and a house to live in with them. Happy in a different way. Because of Concepción, and because of Emilio and little Luiscito and Fortuno and Esteban and all the other children that he played with and slept with and *was* with, always, and not alone sleeping in a cold shed with a pig who woke up snarling and mean.

He had all these friends.

And even—even if there were not to be a party —even then, he was, just now, happy.

He decided he'd pray a little, too, which he didn't do very often, mostly because Father Antonio was always telling him that only by praying night and day did he have the smallest chance of getting to heaven.

"I want a father and mother," he said automatically. "I want them to come and find me and take me away—"

He stopped, and again looked at the chapel full of silent, waiting children. And he had a strange thought. I guess I don't know if I want to have a father and mother who come and take me away, he said to himself, forgetting to pray. To leave all of them, the only people he knew? To go to a strange house, with maybe no other children at all? To be parted forever from Emilio, to sleep all alone by himself in a bed and not have Luiscito snuffling at his side?

To leave Concepción?

Suppose those strangers, his parents, came and decided to take him but wouldn't take Concepción, too? And what about Emilio?

If he couldn't think of something else to pray for, he had better stop praying altogether, except the plain prayer he said every night— that he hoped the other children would be blessed and happy. That Concepción would be blessed and happy. And that Pablo Ortiz was blessed and happy and in heaven in spite of a few lies.

Anything else, and he might be in trouble. He might get answered.

A stir around him announced the arrival of the Cura.

He stood in front of the altar, empty except for two bottles with snapdragons in them, and two white candles that were never lit.

"Good evening, children," said the Cura with a smile. "I have excellent news for you tonight. You are going to be given a party—"

He lifted his hands after a moment to quell the cries and shouts of joy.

"Yes, tomorrow there is to be a party, up in the fields. A picnic. A very very kind lady and gentleman from the United States of America are going to give you this party, and Sister Angela will rehearse you in a song of thanks that you are to sing to them. Now, everybody understands, of course, that you are to be very very good. *Very* good. You must obey the sisters, and not make over-much noise, and behave at all times in a proper manner, so as to bring pride on Casa María."

He paused, looking around. "Children under three," he resumed, "will not be going." He looked at Luiscito, who was just three. "You may go, Luis," he said kindly.

A further pause, while the Cura's glance moved with deliberation along the rows of upturned faces, as if to be certain that all appeared suitably impressed by their responsibility toward this picnic. Finally, his eyes came to rest upon Juan.

Silence, silence.

Father Antonio pushed out his lower lip and seemed to take stock. The children looked at him, holding their breath. Juan, nailed by those grey eyes, shivered in anticipation.

He was not going to be allowed to go. His punishment would be to stay here, while everyone else went up in the fields and had the party. A bitter taste welled in his throat, and his hands and stomach seemed to be coated with ice.

Their eyes locked. Juan's long, narrow, lustrous eyes, and the Cura's small grey ones. And they spoke to each other in wordless scrutiny.

I hate you, said Juan's eyes.

I know you do, Father Antonio's answering gaze seemed to say. *I don't much like you, either.*

The hushed moment extended until the children began to move uneasily, nobody looking at Juan, everybody thinking about him.

"You may go, Juan," Father Antonio went on. "Sister Angela feels that to keep you away would be too great a punishment." He did not say how he felt.

"One of the girls," he continued, "will be obliged to stay with the small children. You, Concepción," he said. "You are to remain here and take care of the babies."

Juan saw Concepción gulp, saw her lip quiver. "Yes, Father," she said.

"I'll bid you good night now," said the Cura, moving his hands in a dusting motion on his black soutane. "Have a good time."

He was gone.

Juan scarcely heard the song that Sister Angela led them through, the song of thanks to the kind and wonderful Señor and Señora who were gracious enough to give them this party for which they would never be able to give sufficient thanks.

When they were finally done, when Sister Angela felt they'd properly learned how to sing a proper song of gratitude, the children filed out of the chapel and then raced to the courtyard to wrest a half hour's play from the fading day.

Juan, seeing that Concepción was not in the courtyard or in the girls' dormitory, went looking for her and found her, at length, in the kitchen, sitting at the thick wooden table, her arms out in front of her, her face quiet and expressionless.

He stood despondently in the doorway, waiting for her to notice him. "Concepción?" he said, when she didn't look up. "Concepción. I won't go, too."

"Juan, don't be silly."

"No, I won't. If you can't go to the party, neither will I. Anyway, he's just doing it to punish me."

Concepción began to laugh. "Doing what to punish you?" she asked, though she knew just what was in his mind.

"Making you stay home with the babies."

She shook her head. "You get the *strangest* ideas."

"No, it's true. He hates me, and he's getting back at me, because he knows I want you to go."

"In the first place, it'd be a funny sort of punishment—to let the person he was punishing go to the party and keep somebody else away from it. And in the second place, he doesn't hate you. And he asked me to stay because last time everybody went out, Consuela stayed with the children, and the time before that, Lola did. It's my turn, see?"

"Yes, but—"

Concepción interrupted. "Juan, can't you see—" She stopped. She'd been going to ask why he couldn't see that he wasn't important enough for the Cura to hate him. Father Antonio probably didn't like Juan much, but that was because Juan could be such a pest. But that was not to hate him. That was just not liking someone, the way you'd not like an insect, or a sliver in your finger. You didn't hate a mosquito, or a sliver. You just found them a nuisance.

But she couldn't say this to self-important little Juan. In some way she couldn't understand, he seemed to depend on the Cura to hate him. She laughed again, briefly, without much amusement, thinking how peculiar it was that Father Antonio meant so much to Juan, while probably the Cura never gave him a thought unless Juan was right under his nose, annoying him.

"Can't I see what?" Juan demanded.

She shrugged. "Oh, that it's only fair for me to stay behind this time. It's my turn," she repeated.

"Then I'm going to stay with you," he said, feeling generous and safe because he knew she'd insist that he go, and she did.

chapter
fourteen

The next morning the children assembled on the street in front of Casa María, and then, with Sister Angela, Consuela, and Lola herding them, walked in double file to the square, where two buses were waiting to take them up to the fields.

Waiting for them also was the North American couple, smiling and excited. The man clutched lots of different-sized colored rubber balls in bright string bags. His wife had a movie camera that she was directing at the oncoming file of orphans.

"Hey, Juan—look, look!" said Emilio, poking Juan in the ribs.

Juan had been scowling at the ground, thinking about how Concepción had hugged him and told him to have a good time. "Now, don't worry about me, Little Turtle," she'd said. "I'll be fine."

Juan, during the night, had had time to decide that Concepción was right—it was only fair for her to stay with the children this time. He'd gone even further, and concluded that she probably wasn't interested in the picnic. She was too old for picnics.

Having got all this settled to his satisfaction, she'd gone and spoiled it by telling him not to worry when he'd already decided not to.

He glanced irritably at Emilio, then followed his friend's pointing finger, and drew his breath.

"It's them," said Emilio, stumbling in his excitement. "It's those people from the square that day."

There they were, the tall *norteamericanos*, dressed in their bright clothes, happy and excited as the children themselves.

At the sight of the camera, the double file from Casa María briefly broke ranks. The children began to wave and grimace and leap about, pushing one another and giggling. It was a sensational experience, being the subjects of a movie, and though they were ordinarily docile and subdued in public, it took Sister Angela several minutes to calm them.

"Señor, Señora," said Sister Angela, when she had her charges quiet again, "these are the children, and they are so grateful and happy at the treat you are about to give them—"

Emilio, not sure where it was supposed to come in, began the song of thanks, found himself singing alone, and stopped abruptly, his face flaming.

Sister Angela smiled at him gently. "That was nice, Emilio, but perhaps we'll save it for later. But now, children, say good morning to Señor and Señora Radway, from the United States of America."

"*Buenas días, buenas días,*" shouted the children. "*Señor y Señora Radway, buenas días!*" Some of them shouted, "Hallo, Hallo, Mister, Mrs."

"And say thank you," Sister Angela directed.

"*Caramba,*" said Fortuno. "We're going to be saying or singing thank you the whole day."

Juan turned to glare at him.

Suddenly, Señora Radway was beside him. She extended a hand. "Remember me?" she said, with a mischievous smile. "How are you, Juan?"

Juan stared upwards in silent adoration. She was still trying to talk Spanish, and her accent was so terrible, she was so wonderful, that all he could do was nod.

Señora Radway turned to Emilio. "*Buenas días, amigo,*" she said.

Emilio, who was beginning to have the most

peculiar idea, put out his scrubbed hand and said, "*Buenas días, Señora.*" He added, with a sly glance at Juan, "We all thank you, very very much we thank you."

"Oh, my gracious," she said. "I really don't want all these thanks. This is fun for us, too, you know. For Mr. Radway and me."

Mr. Radway was getting into the first bus with Consuela, Lola, and half of the children. Mrs. Radway, taking Juan's hand, said, "You come with me. You too—"

"Emilio," said Emilio.

"Yes, of course. Emilio. You and Emilio, Juan, sit with me. You can attempt to improve my Spanish."

She was slim, so all three of them could sit on the same seat in the bus, Juan in the middle, Señora Radway at the window so she could take movies of the town, and Emilio on the aisle.

We're having this picnic, Emilio said to himself, because that lady is crazy about Juan. He pondered this with amazement. Juan, Emilio understood, was the handsomest boy in the orphanage. He, Emilio, was no judge of such things. He only knew that Juan was fun and exciting and sometimes hard to get along with. He was proud to consider himself Juan's best friend. Except for Concepción, of course. But this! Never would he have thought that even Juan could cause a whole picnic to be given, just because he'd smiled at a lady in the square, and talked to her a little.

There was no doubt now in Emilio's mind that this was what had happened. The lady had inquired for Juan at Casa María, had somehow found out that sometimes picnics were given for the orphans, and *pronto*—a picnic was arranged.

In some fashion he didn't understand, this knowledge dimmed the prospect of the party for him. He wasn't jealous of Juan. He'd never been *jealous* of him. It was just—funny. And not entirely fun.

And never before had he seen Juan behaving like this, staring raptly at the Señora, his mouth open a little, laughing and smiling at practically everything she said, although how Juan could understand her terrible Spanish was more than Emilio could figure out. Juan was acting silly, and awfully sweet, and it made Emilio uncomfortable.

Juan, unconscious of Emilio beside him, looked at this beautiful woman taking pictures out of the window as the bus climbed the cobbled hills.

He looked at the houses and the people, trying to see through her blue North American eyes. He hoped she found it grand. All the houses painted so brightly. Blue, pink, green.

The jacaranda trees in purple bloom, bougain-villea and geraniums, pink and orange and red and everywhere. Little burros trotting on their thin legs. Gauchos in from the ranches in their fanciest clothes, on their fine horses. And the people wearing their after-church Sunday air of freedom.

To Juan, the town seemed beautiful this morn-ing in the bright sun, with church bells ringing and burros braying, horses neighing, cocks crow-ing, radios blaring, the warm wind blowing in through the open bus windows.

He gave a little tug on the Señora's sleeve, and she turned to him immediately.

"You like?" he said anxiously.

"Oh, so much, Juan. It's a beautiful little town."

Juan blinked happily, although he had never before thought of the town as little. Emilio jerked, as if he had been bitten by a bee, but Juan didn't notice.

Still, once out of the bus and running, Juan forgot about Señora Radway, as, indeed, all the children immediately forgot their benefactors in the immense and pulsating joy of actually being here, high on the hilltops, on the broad and grassy mesa, free to run in any direction, to shout and shout and shout to the limit of their lungs, to leap and spin and race around like colts or kids in the measureless, sun-drugged fields of the morning.

They broke in all directions, and the soft wind seemed to blow them like straws or balloons across the meadow.

chapter
fifteen

Mr. Radway, who had been eagerly holding aloft the collection of rubber balls in a string bag, lowered them to the ground.

"I thought they'd like to play with these."

"They will, Señor," said Sister Angela. "In a little while."

The three adults watched the swarming galloping mass of children, that seemed directionless, heedless, full of wild springing energy that took them to every corner of the field.

Mrs. Radway was taking moving pictures all the while, and Sister Angela noticed that the camera was aimed consistently at Juan and whoever was with him.

She certainly doesn't mind playing favorites,

Sister Angela thought, hoping the other children wouldn't notice and knowing they would.

"You see," she went on, as they sat on a flat rock to wait for the first heady burst of liberty to spend itself, "they so rarely, almost never, get an opportunity to—to stretch out." She threw her arms wide. "To expand. Do you know what I mean? The orphanage is small, and we have no grounds at all. Just a small courtyard. And the playground we take them to is small, too, and bricked. Believe me, Señor, Señora, if you did nothing, nothing else at all, except take them up here and turn them loose, you would have given them enough.

"Look," she said, and they looked where she directed, at the two older girls racing about, laughing and kicking their heels, among the children. "Lola and Consuela. They are eighteen, and considered 'Sisters' although they have no actual religious vocation. They are girls who stay on in the orphanage, for fear, possibly, of the life they'd have outside. Well, these 'Sisters' seem to be just on a level with the children, do they not, when it comes to being free to run a few hundred yards in any direction?"

Mrs. Radway was biting her lip. "But it seems too *sad*," she said. "To have so little mean so much. Just a chance to run about. It's so *sad*."

Sister Angela made no reply.

"That little boy," Mrs. Radway said after a while. "That one, over there. Juan. Tell me about him."

"What would you like to know?"

"Oh—where he comes from, what will become of him."

"We don't know where he comes from. He's a foundling."

"That glorious baby?" Mrs. Radway exclaimed.

Sister Angela was fleetingly amused at what Juan would say to that. "It happens," she murmured. "As to what will become of him. Who knows?"

"But what does happen to the children when they leave the orphanage?"

"Why, many things, Señora. They go to work. Some of the boys become ranch-hands, or even cowboys, if they learn to ride. They apprentice to carpenters, or tin-workers, if they're lucky. They get jobs at the tile works. The girls marry. Sometimes. Or become maids in the hotels or in the homes of tourists. They work in the embroidery shops, or other shops in town. Some are fortunate and lead good lives, and some fall into evil ways, willingly or unwillingly."

"Juan is divine, isn't he?" Sister Angela frowned at this, and Mrs. Radway said hastily, "I mean—gorgeous, beautiful."

"Yes. Also intelligent, and extremely head-strong."

"Those are qualities that should augur well for his future."

"Let us hope so," said Sister Angela. She rose. "Here comes Manuel with the food and piñatas."

She shook her head in wonderment as one after another of the piñatas was lifted gently from the truck and laid on the ground.

Eight of them. Swans, bulls, lambs, goats.

"My word, how marvelous they are," said Mrs. Radway.

"How generous you are," said Sister Angela, and Manuel and his helper nodded agreement. "The children will never be able to thank you. Nor will I."

"If you're going to do a thing, do it right. That's my motto," said Mr. Radway. "But, believe me, we don't want to be thanked. I mean, for my part, I am thanked. Just watching that scrimmage on the field. We should be thanking you for giving us a chance to do this."

Sister Angela smiled. She was not surprised that there were people in the world like Señor Radway. It just surprised her to meet them occasionally.

"How do they make the piñatas?" Mrs. Radway asked. She was taking movies again, of Juan, who had stopped dashing about and was picking field flowers, and also of the piñatas, of Manuel and his helper, who were setting up a table of boards across sawhorses. Now she turned the camera on Sister Angela, who pretended not to notice, though she felt like bridling, as the children had.

"They make a clay—how would you say? A clay barrel," she said. "And fill it with little toys, balloons, candy, fruit, nuts. And then the form, of the swan or the lamb, or whatever, is made of tissue paper ribbons around it."

"Whoever made these is an artist," said Mr. Radway.

"I've always loved them," said Sister Angela. "Loved looking at them," she added thoughtfully.

The children had spied the piñatas and, pounding like a herd of ponies, had made a dash, halting suddenly to stand in a silent, awed circle, looking at this feast of promise.

The eight piñatas, dazzling in their size and beauty. The table, which Manuel and his helper were gradually piling with sandwiches, fruit, nuts, and two enormous cakes, frosted, and decorated with frosting flowers of different colors. At either end of the table were great galvanized buckets in which bottles of soft drinks nestled in ice.

Most of the children were panting from nearly

half an hour's uninterrupted racing about. All of them were thirsty. Not one asked for a drink, or moved a step forward, or crowded from the rear.

They simply stood and waited, their eyes shining and trustful.

Mrs. Radway said miserably, "Why are they so well-behaved? It isn't natural."

"It's natural to our children," said Sister Angela. "You can see that with only Lola, Consuela, and myself, we could scarcely bring nearly eighty children on an outing if they were not well-behaved."

"Oh, yes. I see. I know. But still—" Mrs. Radway sighed. "Couldn't they have a drink now?"

"If that's what you wish."

"I was thinking more of what the children might wish," the woman said sharply. She added, "Forgive me. I sound awful. It's just that —just that—" She shook her head. "I don't know what I mean. But do let's let them have a drink."

Oh, how sweet, how sharp, how tingling and happy to the throat was the cold drink!

Juan relished the chill feeling of the glass bottleneck against his lips and teeth. He closed his eyes as the delicious fluid filled his mouth, then put back his head and swallowed slowly, blissfully, licking his lips between each sip. Halfway through the bottle, he stopped drinking to give Mrs. Radway such a look of lively pleasure that she started toward him, her eyes brimming.

"Sit with me a bit," she said. And then, "You, too—Emilio."

But Emilio retreated a few steps, then turned and ran awkwardly away, holding his thumb over the top of his bottle so as not to lose any of the soft drink.

Mrs. Radway looked after him. "Why did he do that?"

Juan, who was glad Emilio had gone, just shrugged.

"The piñatas, Señora," he said. "And the table, all full of beautiful things. I like to look at them."

"Do you, Juan?" she said, smiling down at him. The affection in her eyes seemed to envelop him in warmth. "Tell me something about yourself, won't you?"

"About myself, Señora?" Juan said happily. It was an unusual invitation, and although he noticed that a soccer game, a real game with plenty of running room and somebody keeping score, was going on, he gave himself over to Señora Radway, who wanted to know about him, and was the only person besides Concepción who ever had.

chapter

sixteen

They made a tremendous effort to understand each other. Juan couldn't help laughing at her accent and at all the mistakes she made, but the way she laughed with him made him feel grown-up and protective.

He looked at her approvingly, with open admiration. Today she had her mango-hair tied back with a green ribbon. She wore a yellow dress and green bracelets above her elbow. He guessed he'd never seen anybody so beautiful before in his life.

One part of him was saying that it was wrong for her to pay all her attention to him, and that was why Emilio was so sulky. But a stronger part responded with such joy to this attention that he could not make himself leave her.

"What do you do all day, Juanito?" she asked, sending a little thrill throughout his body. When had anyone, even Concepción, ever called him Juanito?

He shrugged carelessly, as though to deny that shiver of tenderness, of sweetness. Not thinking it all through, he still knew that it was best not to love being loved this way by someone who would be gone in a day, or a week, probably never to come back.

"Nothing, Señora. I mean, school. We go to school in the morning, and learn about Mexico and its heroes and how to read and write. And every morning at six o'clock we go to mass."

"At six o'clock? Every morning?"

He nodded. "Some mornings it's cold. And some mornings," he added deliberately, "it's wet. Awfully wet. My feet," he added slowly, as if uncertain whether to say it or not, but going ahead, "my feet get wet."

"But don't you have rubbers, or boots?"

"No," he said flatly.

He studied her with calculating eyes. This might be a way, he thought craftily, to—

Then, with a rush of real emotion, he said, "It doesn't matter, Señora. Truly, it doesn't matter."

She was so beautiful, so kind, so understanding. He was ashamed of himself, and of what he had thought to do. Hurrying on, to distract her, he said, "We go to the playground sometimes. And Concepción—that's my friend, Concepción, who is not here because she had to stay with the babies—Concepción takes Emilio and me to the square sometimes. To the Bean Bank. That is when we met you, Señora, when we were going to the Bean Bank for rice."

"To the Bean Bank for rice?"

Then he had to tell her what the Bean Bank was, and how nice Señor Sautello was, and how beautiful the bins of beans. He told her about Emilio.

"He's clumsy," Juan said fondly. "He's my best friend, too. Besides Concepción. And he has a personal possession."

"A what?"

"A personal possession, Señora. Something that is his own and nobody else's. It's a picture of his mother and father in a gold frame. It's in the closet where people who have personal possessions—have them. In the closet. They can look when they want to."

"And what is yours, Juanito? What is your personal possession?"

"I don't have one," he said hurriedly. "And I had another friend, Pablo Ortiz. He would have had such a good time up here today. He used to be the best soccer player in Casa María. Now I am."

"Where is Pablo?"

"In heaven, I guess, Señora."

"Oh. Oh, I'm sorry."

"I hope Pablo isn't."

He was beginning to get restless, his legs trembling with the need to be in the soccer game, but then she said, "Tell me, Juan. What do you want most in the world?"

Until today, he might have said, "A picnic in the fields." But now he was having that, and it would soon be over, so he said without hesitation, "A pair of red rubber boots."

She looked as if she hadn't heard correctly, then repeated in a surprised, a disappointed tone, "Red rubber boots?"

Juan nodded eagerly, not able to help himself. "Such a pair of boots as I saw on a *gringo*—I mean, tourist—boy, running through the rain one day. Like, Señora, like—boots that ran of themselves, taking the boy with them through the puddles and the rain. Oh, there is just such a pair of boots in the market, Señora. I saw them, hanging there, red like firecrackers—"

"But Juan," she protested. "You can't want a pair of boots more than anything else in the whole world!"

104

Juan said firmly that he did.

"But I should think—that is, it seems to me, Juanito, that you'd like to have—" She hesitated, then blurted, the way a child would when he had to say something better left unsaid. "Why don't you want *parents* more than anything else in the world?"

Juan looked at her almost coldly. "Señora, I am not an orphan."

"But—"

"My parents, my mamacita and papá, have left me here only while they travel. My father must travel for his business, which is very important and dangerous, and they do not wish to risk me, their son. So I stay here until they come back." He stood up. "It is only for a little while."

Then he relented and smiled at her. She was very kind and pretty and it was not her fault she thought he was an orphan. "I must go play in the game, Señora. *Adios.*"

Mrs. Radway turned perplexedly to Sister Angela, who had come up to them during Juan's outline of his position.

"That's not true, is it? What he says?"

Sister Angela shook her head.

"Juan dreams. He makes things up for himself. Many of the children do. Father Antonio—" She broke off. She'd been about to say that the Cura disapproved this sort of dreaming, especially in Juan, who carried it to unheard of, possibly even wicked, lengths. Most of the children, faced with it, would admit that their fancies were fantasy and not fact. But Juan—never. Faced with it, he'd just invent something more extreme.

She could not, of course, discuss Father Antonio with a visitor. The Cura called Juan a liar, Sister Angela and Concepción thought him a desperate dreamer, but none of that concerned Señora Radway, who was here today and would be gone tomorrow.

To the great delight of the children, Mr. Radway had flung himself into the soccer game. Nearly as awkward as Emilio, he dashed about, laughing as hard as the children at his own clumsiness.

Sister Angela was enchanted with him.

"See," she said to the woman beside her. "They are treating him as they do Emilio, or the littlest children. Watch."

Indeed, it became clear to anyone watching that the boys and most of the girls played a fast hard game, with speed and accuracy, yet every now and then someone would see to it that Emilio, or Mr. Radway, or some small participant, like Luiscito, had an opportunity to hit the ball, too, and this was done by sending it in a lazy arc that couldn't possibly be missed.

"They look out for one another, don't they?" Mrs. Radway said.

Sister Angela nodded. "They are all the family they have. Sometimes, Señora, I think they are better off, and happier, in Casa María than many of them would be in families of their own."

"Do many of them get adopted?"

"Why, no. No. It is almost unheard of. Mexico —we are not a rich nation. People cannot afford to adopt children. They already have so many of their own."

"But there are rich families."

"They, too, have children of their own. Or, if not of their very own, there are always multitudes of relatives and *their* children. No, an orphan remains an orphan here," she said decisively.

"Don't—don't you have Americans—I mean, North Americans—who would want to take one of the children?"

"But they wouldn't be permitted, Señora," said Sister Angela in astonishment.

"Not permitted?"

"Not possibly. We Mexicans do not allow our children to be taken away from us."

"But if somebody could give a child a good home, and love?"

"Out of the question, Señora."

Mrs. Radway started to say something more,

perhaps even to call this reasoning into question, but at Sister Angela's expression, she held her tongue.

She and her husband loved Mexico, but she thought they would never, no matter how often they visited, no matter if one day they came and lived there, never would they understand it.

"The game would go on forever, Señora," Sister Angela said. "Shall we interrupt it for lunch?"

chapter
seventeen

After lunch, after the sandwiches and the cakes and fruits had disappeared, leaving not a crumb or an apple seed for inquiring birds, the first piñata was strung between two trees and the high point of the day was upon them.

First, a swan. A large, pink, shimmering swan, that rose and fell as Manuel, with the rope, lowered it, raised it, to the accompaniment of shrieking and laughter from the children.

Emilio had been blindfolded and given a stick, and he was wildly swinging in an eyeless attempt to shatter the hovering, rosy bird. Once he tapped it, and the children roared encouragement, but then he wandered out of its ken altogether. Consuela gently guided him back in the right direction and Manuel, with a smile,

lowered the piñata to a point where with one great whack Emilio managed to crack the swan's clay body.

As the favors and balloons and little apples and toys came spilling out, the mangled swan bounded overhead and the children scrambled wildly over the ground, grabbing at the goodies, stuffing their mouths, their pockets, all the while shouting and laughing.

Sister Angela, waiting for Manuel to string up the second piñata, a great black bull with a yellow collar and sequin eyes, said thoughtfully to Mr. Radway, "There is something about piñatas that brings out—" She shook her head and fell silent.

Brings out the worst in people, Mr. Radway finished silently. It was something he'd often thought. You watched these beautiful things hacked and destroyed, watched the mindless melee that went on underneath the battered and broken thing that had been so lovely, so shortly before, and wondered about people. Not just children. People. Not just Mexicans and piñatas. People. Everywhere. Wanting to destroy.

He and Sister Angela exchanged glances, and although his wife had asked him to get movies of this rite, the camera remained on a rock. No doubt later he'd regret the lack of those pictures. The ceremony was, after all, a custom of

the country and, as such, interesting. But he
didn't want to take pictures of it, and he didn't.

Mrs. Radway, at a distance, was watching
Juan, whom she could have loved. After a long
time, she looked away.

chapter
eighteen

Juan came home with one pocket full of nuts, the other bulging with small apples and two red balloons. He had the long pink tissue-paper tail of the swan, stuck here and there with a sequin, and the field flowers that folded limply over his hand.

"Here," he said to Concepción. "These are for you."

"Why, Juan," she said happily. "They're beautiful. I love them."

"The swan tail's okay, but I guess I picked the flowers too early."

"I love them," she said again, looking at the wilted little mass of stems and tired blossoms.

"These, too," he said, giving her some nuts and apples.

"Did you miss me?"

Juan nodded vigorously. "Oh, yes, Concepción. I missed you very very much. I thought about you all the time."

Although, in fact, he hadn't thought of her at all except briefly when telling Señora Radway about her, Juan now realized, seeing Concepción, that he'd been aware of her absence throughout the afternoon. It would have been more fun with her there.

"I broke my piñata first whack. A lamb, it was. You should have seen me, Concepción."

"I think I did see you, I thought about you so hard," she said wistfully. "Was it lots of fun? Tell me about it. Did you all sing your song nicely? What did you have to eat?"

Juan told her, with much detail, about the wide and reaching fields, about the soccer game and the great table and the beautiful decorated cakes. He described each piñata carefully, not neglecting to tell which lucky person had finally broken which one. He told how Señor Radway had tried to play soccer with them, and had been so happy when somebody let him get his foot on the ball, though he'd never succeeded in hitting it with his head.

"*Muy sympático*, the Señor," said Juan.

"And the Señora?" Concepción said, a little frostily. "Was she *muy sympática*, also?

"She was okay," he said carelessly, and went back to describing the lunch, and what a great success their thank-you song had been.

A few days later a package arrived at Casa María, for Juan.

"For Juan?" said Sister Angela to Manuel, who had brought it. "Which Juan? We have seven."

"It's from that Señora Radway," said Manuel, lifting his shoulders. "She said you'd know who it was for. She said she didn't know his last name, but you'd know who she meant."

"But she can't—but to send a present to just one child?" said Sister Angela. "Even Señora Radway wouldn't be so thoughtless."

"Oh, she's ordered a lot of rice and candy for the Casa," said Manuel. "Sautello is sending it over later. She also told me that she knew you wouldn't be too pleased, but you'd have to forgive her for this—" He gestured at the package. "She said she couldn't help herself."

"You'll have to return it, Manuel."

"No possibility. They're gone. She and Señor Radway left last night."

Sister Angela turned the package around, looking from it to Manuel in a perplexed and doubtful way. "What shall I do?" she murmured.

Manuel had nothing to offer. He got in his truck and drove off.

Consuela was going by the office door, and Sister Angela called to her, "Find Concepción for me, will you please, and ask her to come here."

While she waited, she looked at the package on her desk as if it represented a betrayal. How could Señora Radway have done such an inconsiderate thing? Then, recalling Señora Radway's actions at the picnic, her unapologetic singling out of Juan, her questions about adoption, her taking movies of Juan as if the other children were supernumerary, she could readily believe that Señora Radway would do just this.

But what could she, Sister Angela, do now? Discard the thing? That was not possible. It was addressed to Juan. It was his. It was the first thing that had ever been meant for him alone.

"It's not mine to dispose of," Sister Angela muttered irritably. She'd never been faced with precisely such a difficulty before. To be sure, some of the children got a present from a relative now and then. Some of the children had personal things they'd brought with them, things that were kept for them in a cupboard in the hall.

But a present from a stranger to just one child? No, it was unforgivable.

116

"What shall we do?" she asked, when Concepción had entered and had the package explained to her. "To pick one child out of eighty to give a present to! How self-indulgent of her."

"Why Juan? He practically didn't notice her, did he? He told me he'd hardly seen her. I think he told me that," Concepción added, not sure now.

"Well, that wasn't the way of it. She picked him out, and only by the greatest effort did she pay attention to anyone else. Which—" She stopped, looking closely at Concepción. "Please, please," she said sharply. "Do not get jealous and emotional, Concepción. Or, in any case, not just now. You must help me with this—this dilemma."

Concepción looked stubborn and disobliging. She said nothing.

"Concepción," Sister Angela entreated. "You are a grown-up, just about a grown-up, person. Juan is a little boy. Can't you see how he'd be pleased at the attentions of a woman like Señora Radway? She was obviously most taken with him, and how could a child resist that? I must say, he showed more tact, more consideration for you, in keeping this to himself than I'd have expected."

Concepción's lip quivered.

"Oh, my," said Sister Angela wearily. "What

do you want of him? That every breath he draws should be sanctified to you?"

Concepción cried out. "Oh no, Sister. Oh, no. I want only—that he should be happy."

"Then act as if that's what you want," Sister Angela snapped. "Forgive me. I must remember that you are not, after all, entirely grown. And that you feel as if Juan were your own. But don't be jealous, Concepción. Guard against this terrible, dreadful, emotion. It leads only to pain on every side. If you truly love Juan, you will not begrudge him affection from any quarter."

"I do truly love him."

"Of course you do. But how could Señora Radway's feeling for him in any way affect his for you? Think, Concepción. *Think.*"

Concepción drew a deep breath, and nodded. "You are right, Sister Angela. You are, of course, right."

That Sister Angela was right did little to calm the jealousy that tore at Concepción like a clawed animal. Oh, she could never, *never*, begrudge affection from someone else toward Juan, toward her own Little Turtle. She wanted him to be loved. But not by a rich and beautiful North American who could offer him things Concepción could not.

"The next thing," she said, choking, "the next thing will be she'll want to adopt him."

Sister Angela said nothing, and after a moment Concepción, who hadn't taken her own remark seriously, turned her attention to the box on the desk.

She glared at it, this package containing a pair of red rubber boots for Juan.

chapter
nineteen

Concepción didn't have to look inside to know what this present contained. If Señora Radway had got so close to Juan, had spent so much time with him, then she'd found out he wanted a pair of red rubber boots, because sooner or later, and usually sooner, everyone who came near him heard about the boots.

So now he had them. So now the red rubber boots were a fact. Just because Señora Radway could buy what she wanted to, because she wanted to. Like that.

All at once, Concepción began to cry.

Sister Angela started up and put her arms around the sobbing girl. "Forgive me, Concepción. I was harsh with you."

"It isn't that, Sister. It isn't that at all! Oh,

Sister Angela, for months and months I have been trying to save, from what Casa María gives me to work in the kitchen, enough to buy Juan a pair of boots. But it would take another year, another two years. And now—and now—" She waved her hand at the box. "And now she just does it, just *buys* them, just like that. And yesterday she gave him a picnic in the fields, and oh, it isn't fair, it isn't fair!"

Knowing that there is no answer to *"It isn't fair!"* Sister Angela patted the thin shoulders and waited for the tears to stop. They did, after a while. Sniffling, Concepción looked up and tried to smile.

"This still leaves us with the problem of what to do with this present, these boots. If it is boots. Whatever it is," Sister Angela said.

"It's boots," Concepción said gloomily.

"How can I tell the children that the kind people who gave them the picnic have selected one child for special attention? It seems to me it would remove the flavor, the joy of recalling the party. I believe," she said, as if arriving at a decision, "I shall just put the thing away and say nothing about it."

"Oh, but—"

"But what, Concepción? I should think such a solution would please you."

"But he wants them so *badly,* Sister. It would

mean so much to him."

Even jealousy couldn't stop Concepción from wanting anything, everything, for Juan. Seeing this, Sister Angela was touched, and a little sad. Concepción was going to be one of those people who gave too ardently for thanks. In a way, that was wonderful, for Concepción and those she would love. And yet, Sister Angela found it pitiable.

"I suppose," she said slowly, "that since some of the other children have small personal possessions, we could let Juan have the boots. Do you think we could swear him to secrecy? Ask him not to let the other children know where they came from?"

"They'd find out. They find out everything. Including," Concepción added with a downward droop to her mouth, "how things just aren't fair in this life."

They were silent for a moment, and then Concepción said suddenly, "What about Father Antonio? Maybe he won't let Juan have the boots," she went on in an excited tone. "Maybe he'll—"

"Concepción! You will please not fall into Juan's fantasy of the Cura as his enemy. Father Antonio doesn't dote on Juan, to be sure. But would you dote on Juan, if you were the Cura?"

Concepción giggled. "I'd find it easier to dote on someone else," she admitted.

"Father Antonio may not love Juan, but he is not a cruel man. I believe," Sister Angela added, "he'd prefer not to be consulted at all in this case. I'm afraid the decision must be entirely ours, and we seem to be taking up the day making it. Oh, dear," she said vexedly. "What a lot of trouble this Señora Radway is causing, with her thoughtless thoughtfulness."

They talked, saying the same thing in various ways, trying to come to a conclusion they both knew had already been arrived at.

"All right," said Sister Angela with a sober air. "I suppose we might as well get it over with. Go and find him, Concepción."

chapter
twenty

Juan came bounding into the room in front of Concepción, who trailed unhappily after him. His brown eyes were blazing.

"Sister Angela!" he shouted. "Concepción says there is a *package* for me. Is that true?"

"Would Concepción say such a thing if it were not true?"

Juan disregarded that. He was staring at the box on the desk, taking in its shape, its size. He looked from Sister Angela to Concepción, hardly breathing.

"That's it?" he said finally, in a low, nervous voice. "That's for me?"

"Yes, Juan. Señora Radway sent it. She and the Señor have ordered rice and candy for the entire Casa. But this is just for you. The Señor and Señora," she added, "have left."

Juan seemed not to hear. He put his hand out, drew it back. He felt dizzy. Never in his whole life had he got a package before, and he somehow couldn't relate it to the people who had sent it. He wondered if he really wanted to open it. It was wrapped in bright paper and tied with a ribbon and it surely—surely—contained—

In there, in that wrapped box, was a pair of red rubber boots. For him, Juan. He was as close as opening a package to a pair of boots of his own.

Still he did nothing but stare at the thing on the desk. This thing that was boots, that was his. "Only me?" he said finally. "Nobody else got something?"

"Rice and candy, for everybody," Sister Angela reminded him.

"But a package only for me?"

"Yes."

All at once Juan dove at it, the way he'd pounced on the falling contents of the piñatas. He tore the paper and ribbon ruthlessly, tossed the cover off the box, and then stood still again, just looking.

There they lay, a pair of boots just like those in the market, just like those on the tourist boy. Red as firecrackers and—slowly, trembling a little, he tried them on—and *just his size*.

He stood in his boots and looked at Concepción and Sister Angela and tried to speak but could not, so he turned and walked out of the room, stumbling a little, filled with awe.

He wore them all day. It meant he couldn't play soccer because the boots made him clumsy. His feet began to feel hot and slippery. He began to be angry because nobody talked about them. Everybody looked at the boots on his feet and nobody, not even Emilio, said, "Hey, Juan, where'd you get the boots?"

Because they all knew where the boots had come from. From the Señora, who, with the Señor, had given them their wonderful party in the fields, but had given only Juan a present, a real present.

At lunch, everybody got two pieces of candy, and Father Antonio told them that there would be enough so that candy would be given them at lunch every day for two weeks. He also told them that the kind North Americans had ordered a great quantity of rice for Casa María, for which they must all be grateful and say thank you in their prayers. Since they ate rice all the time, this didn't interest them the way it did Sister Angela and Father Antonio, and most of them forgot to say anything about rice in their prayers.

Juan wore his boots to church, to class, to

chapel, to the yard, where he stood against the wall watching the soccer game progress. Finally he wore them to bed.

He said his prayers, remembering to include Señor and Señora Radway in them. (For several nights thereafter he put them in, just after Pablo Ortiz, but gradually forgot.)

The boots were difficult to sleep in, but he managed.

In the morning he found that he was all alone on the mattress.

"Hey, Emilio," he said, sitting up, seeing Emilio and Luiscito on the mattress next to his, so that there were four of them there and only himself here. "Hey, Emilio, Luiscito, how come you're over there?"

"You kicked us," Emilio said, not coldly or angrily, just by way of explanation.

"With those boots," said Luiscito.

The word had been said, the boots had been mentioned. And now all the children looked at Juan to find out what he would say.

Juan leaned against the wall, his legs stretched out before him, the brilliant boots—the most noticeable adornment that had ever been seen in the boys' dormitory—winking and gleaming on his feet.

He looked slowly around at his friends, who stared solemnly, silently back. Only Luiscito

could be heard. He sobbed softly, saying over and over, "Nobody else got something. Nobody else got nothing."

But Luiscito was only three, and he was the only one who made a sound.

Juan lifted his eyes and stared at Christ, riding his cloud far up on the grey and cracked and peeling wall. He looked at the cockroach that always seemed to be walking around up there.

Slowly he leaned over, and slowly, carefully, he removed his boots. First the right one, then the left one. His feet, out in the air once more, seemed to wriggle of their own accord.

What he was going to do was—he was going to ask Sister Angela to put his boots, his treasure, his personal possession, in the closet with Fortuno's three-quarter violin and Emilio's picture of his parents in their gold frame, and some other private and personal possessions. And once in a while he would look at them. But he thought he wouldn't wear them.

Because it turned out that he showed too much, wearing the boots. It turned out that even if nobody said anything (Well, Luiscito was still saying something but he was only three and didn't count), even if nobody *said* to him, "How come you got a present when nobody else did?" he felt funny. As if, somehow, he'd cheated. Which he hadn't. He didn't know why he'd got a present when no one else had. Or, he supposed he knew why, but it wasn't his fault if the Señora had liked him so much and he had just happened to mention the boots to her. It had just happened, that was all.

He guessed he'd always remember the dizzying, the nearly scaring joy of seeing that package, of tearing it open to find the red shining glorious rubber boots lying there, all for him. But he guessed, too, that the most fun was over now.

Yes, the boots would make him feel peculiar, different. And he didn't want to feel that way. He didn't *think* he wanted to feel that way.

"I'm going to save them," he announced. "When my papá and my mamacita come to get me, then I'll wear them. When I go away."

Your feet will be as big as the Cura's by then, thought Emilio. But he didn't say it.

"That's what I'll do," Juan repeated. "Wear them when I go away with my mother and father."

He knew what they were thinking. That he no more had a mother and father than they did. Which showed how much they knew. His parents were there, somewhere in the world, looking for him, and one day they'd find him. When that day came, he'd leave Casa María forever. He'd say good-bye to his friends, and to Sister

Angela, but not to Father Antonio, and then he'd put on his red rubber boots and go, with Concepción, to his new home.

But all that was a long way off, he thought with relief. It was nothing he had to think about now. For now, he had his friends, and a pair of boots besides, and with the boots safely in the cupboard, he'd be able to play soccer again, and that was very good.

And, maybe, if when the rainy season came again and his parents still had not found him—why then, he might just, just *might*, get the boots out of the cupboard.

They were, after all, *his* boots.

Format by Phoebe Amsterdam
Set in 12/15 Antique No. 1
Composed by Haddon Craftsmen, Inc.
Printed by Murray Printing Co.
Harper & Row, Publishers, Inc.